Moses Hull

Your Answer or Your Life

The riddle propounded by the American Sphinx

Moses Hull

Your Answer or Your Life
The riddle propounded by the American Sphinx

ISBN/EAN: 9783337390136

Printed in Europe, USA, Canada, Australia, Japan

Cover: Foto ©Andreas Hilbeck / pixelio.de

More available books at **www.hansebooks.com**

YOUR ANSWER

—or—

YOUR LIFE,

—or—

The Riddle Propounded by the American Sphinx.

BY

MOSES HULL,

AUTHOR OF "THE QUESTION SETTLED," "THE CONTRAST BETWEEN EVANGELICALISM AND SPIRITUALISM," "WHICH, SPIRITUALISM OR CHRISTIANITY?" "JOAN, THE HEROINE OF ORLEANS," "THE IRREPRESSIBLE CONFLICT," "THE DECAY OF INSTITUTIONS," "BIBLICAL AND MODERN MEDIUMSHIP," AND SEVERAL OTHER WORKS ON REFORMATORY SUBJECTS.

DES MOINES, IOWA
MOSES HULL & CO.
1888.

MOSES HULL.

PREFACE.

"A penny for your thoughts," rang out upon the air one cool morning as I walked, in profound meditation, supposing myself to be entirely alone. "They would this morning fill a dozen issues of the *Chicago Times*," was my response. "If I could only be turned wrong side out, and my thoughts could be known and read of all men as they force themselves upon my own attention, I would have some hope for our country, but, alas!"—"O, yes, I know what you are going to say; the drouth, yes, it's rather hard on Kansas farmers, but we'll pull through somehow." "No," said I, "I was thinking of those innocent men who are to be legally murdered next week because of the sins of the people. This is not our first act of injustice, I wonder if it is not nearly the last one. As surely as

Sodom and Gomorrah were to rise in judgment against the cities of Judea, so sure must the old monarchies rise in judgment against our government." The conversation thus sprung upon me culminated in several long talks, in each of which I was urged, as was one of old, to "write the vision and make it plain upon tables that he may run that readeth it." Hab. ii:2.

There is little that is original in this book, I have striven simply to point out some of the dangers we are under, and to signify the way of escape. If this *brochure* shall open a few pair of eyes and set a few men and women to pointing out the way and all to fleeing from "The City of Destruction," I shall be glad; if not, I shall at least have the satisfaction of knowing I did all in my power to show America her danger.

MOSES HULL.

Des Moines, Iowa, June 1, 1888.

CONTENTS.

CONTENTS.

CHAPTER I.

THE RISE AND FALL OF NATIONS.

A WONDER OF THE WORLD.—DIMENSIONS OF THE SPHINX.—
ITS RIDDLE.—A SUPPOSED ANSWER.—SUICIDE OF NATIONS.
—EVIDENCES OF EGYPT'S FORMER CIVILIZATION.—"CLEO-
PATRA'S NEEDLES."—POMPEY'S PILLAR.—MONOLITH AT
MEMNON.—THE PYRAMIDS.—WHY HAS EGYPT'S CIVILIZA-
TION FALLEN?—ZOROASTER MORALS.—THE FIRST BOARD
OF TRADE.—WHY SHE DIED.—ROME.—WHAT MADE HER
GREAT?—WHY DID SHE FALL?—EXTRACT FROM AN ELO-
QUENT SERMON.—HISTORICAL FACTS.—CONCLUSION.

If the reader of these pages wishes to see fully illustrated the evidences that nations fall and go into desolation, let him take a trip on the Nile, the only river in Egypt, from Alexandria to Ipsamboul. There he will at once see the evidences of a former grandeur not seen elsewhere in the world, and of a present desolation so sickening, at least, as to stimulate in him feelings akin to those so grandly expressed by the eloquent M. Volney, when journeying among its desolations.

Across from Cairo, a comparatively modern city, one hundred and thirty-five miles up the Nile, and a little back from the river, stands one of the wonders of the world. It is a huge stone sculptured out in

the likeness of a lion and a woman; that is, it is a
lion's body with a woman's head. This monolith,
with its wide-open eyes, has, it is supposed by some,
stood there over *fifteen thousand years*, not only to
watch the passers-by, but to watch the birth, growth,
old age and death of nations. It is itself, an evidence
of a huge, barbaric civilization of an hundred centuries in the past. It stands *seventy-five* feet up in
the air; its huge body lies *one hundred and forty*
feet on the ground, with itspaws extending *fifty feet*
in front, thus making it *one hundred and ninety*
feet in length. This monster is called the Egyptian
Sphinx; tradition gives as the reason why it was
called "the sphinx," which is merely the Greek word
for "strangler," a habit it had of propounding a riddle, to all who came that way, and its other and worse
habit of strangling to death all who could not solve
its riddle.

May there not in this, as in most mythological
tales, be a shading of truth? I have somewhere
seen this interpretation. The question, or riddle
propounded by the Egyptian Sphinx was: "How can
you maintain your present civilization?" Could
the question have been properly answered, Egypt
could have continued all she ever was, and her glory
would not only have covered the valley of the Nile,
from Nubia to the Mediterranean, but would have
extended until its law would have put new life into

all other nations, and no decay of nations would ever have been known. Be that as it may, nations are not born to live out a puny, sickly, short existence, and then die of premature old age. The history of dead nations proves them generally to have committed suicide. No especial providence ever yet killed a nation or a person.

It is hardly within my present province to give an extended history of Egypt's former greatness and present desolation; yet, a few words may show from what heights a nation may fall.

The river Nile, by its slow process, has, in some places, deposited *seventy-five* feet of earth over some of the evidences of that country's gigantic civilization. At that depth pottery has been found carefully laid away by the dish-washers of over an hundred centuries ago. There has been discovered evidences that way back in pre-historic times, the inhabitants of the Nile valley could harden copper so hard that it would shave a piece of the hardest steel with the comparative ease with which one whittles a piece of castile soap with a butcher knife. In those days glass was made as malleable as iron is to-day. Astronomical and philosophical instruments show that an astonishing amount of wisdom had been accumulated in that direction.

At Alexandria once stood the same Cleopatra's Needles, one of which now stands in Central Park, New

York; the other on the Thames. One of the greatest feats of modern engineering was to get those great monuments from Egypt, the one to London and the other to New York, and erect them where they now stand; yet the ancient Egyptians, by some means, cut those monoliths out of the living rock, and moved them by land *eight hundred miles*, and set them up at the mouth of the Nile.

Cleopatra's Needle is a small affair compared with Pompey's Pillar, which stands erect to-day, at Alexandria. The world has never before or since seen such a single shaft as that. How this huge stone, *one hundred and fourteen feet high* and *eleven feet* in diameter, *sixteen feet* through the plynth and abachus, was brought from the quarries of Syenne and erected, is a question which modern engineering has asked a thousand times, but never answered.

The image at Memnon, called the Memnoniam, in Thebes surpasses either of the former shafts as Niagra surpasses a brooklet. This huge monster, "the beloved of Ammon," carved in the shape of a man, once stood erect, guarding the entrance to the temple of Memnon. It is over *ninety feet* high, the ear is *three feet long;* it is *twenty-two* feet from the knee to the plant of the boot and is estimated to weigh *thirty thousand tons*. How was it removed to Thebes? How set up? How thrown down?

The huge Pyramid of Cheops, covering thirteen

and a half acres and extending *four hundred and eighty* feet in the air is another monument of the power and intelligence of the people of *fifteen thousand* years ago, as is proved by the precession of the equinoxes. The eye in the center of this huge pile of stones, looking at the north star, tells very definitely when it was builded, and gives something of an idea of the knowledge of astronomy in that early age of the world.

Translations from the hieroglyphics, on their temples and tombs, show something of the moral status of that ancient people. Why should such civilization crumble into the dust? It is said that nations, as men, are born to grow, to thrive, to dwindle, to decay, and finally to die. This statement is based on observation; but is there any necessity for nations dying? Why should nations die? Nay, is not their death, in most cases, suicide?

I have read the history of the downfall of no nation, that did not die of its own follies and sins. God never killed a nation. Moses told Israel if they would be obedient they should "eat the fat of the land;" otherwise, they should be destroyed.

Who has not heard of the crimes against the producing classes committed in that giant gamblers' den, known as the "Board of Trade," in America, but turn back to Egypt and view there the seed out of which all such institutions have grown. Zo-

roaster, the Persian Moses, who lived as far back, at
least, as the days when the Hebrew Moses led his
brothers and sisters out of Egypt, seemed to have a
foresight that such gamblers' nests as Boards of
Trade would be hatched out, so he said:

"Who ever buys grain when it is cheap and holds it
from the people to make it dear, commits the worst of
all sins, for he commits the sin that leads to all others."

He was right, star ation and the impossibility of
getting the wherewim to supply the wants of a
hungry wife and children will lead loving and true
husbands and fathers into all manner of crime.
The sin, in such cases, lies at the door of gamblers,
known as "speculators."

In Egypt the Board of Trade was born, and out
of that Board of Trade was hatched the swarm of
crimes which causes Egypt to-day to keep a per-
petual Sabbath, from Ipsamboul to Alexandria.
Three thousand years ago an Israelite proposed to
the reigning monarch to corner all the corn there
was in Egypt; be it remembered, corn is a generic
term, and signifies grain. This struck Pharaoh
as being a good move. So when he got the grain
"cornered," the people who raised it came to this
Board of Trade, and paid in money, such prices as
were demanded. Soon, however, their money was
gone, then what was to be done? They were in-
formed that they could bring their cattle [chattels]

and trade them for grain. This source of revenue was also soon exhausted, and they were then told that the supply of grain had not run out, they could have grain for their lands.

When their land and everything else had passed into the hands of these robbers, the people could do nothing else than sell themselves for something to eat.

Thus, the Board of Trade very soon cornered all the wealth of the country, insomuch that *three* per cent. of Egypt's citizens owned *ninety-seven* per cent. of her wealth, leaving *ninety-seven* per cent. of her citizens with but *three* per cent. of her wealth. The unequal distribution of her wealth, like the unequal circulation of blood through the human system, caused apoplexy, from which she, though the richest country on earth, never recovered.

The history of Egypt is our example; could we learn from the things she has suffered, we might be saved from a similar fate.

What I have said of Egypt is equally true of Rome. She was once the grandest and most democratic nation on the earth. Her wealth was distributed among the multitude, and, of course, her people were happy. The land was divided among the millions. Her greatest warriors and greatest senators were still greater farmers. *Eighty-five* per cent. of the population were land-owners, and felt that they had something to fight for, and were therefore the most invincible soldiers the world had ever seen.

Neibhur, the great German historian, says:

"To what, more than to her system of colonization, a branch of her agrarian scheme, was she [Rome] indebted for the security and extention of her frontier? A host of warriors were trained up ready to take the field at the call of their country, yet no less ready to exchange the sword for the plowshare. It is not, however, in a military point of view that the value of these institutions is evident. They were of no less domestic importance in providing against the phenomena so frequently met with in great cities, of the squalid indigence by the side of the most profuse extravagance."

Rev. Gilbert De LaMatyr, in one of his sermons, uses the following eloquent language:

"With the history of mighty Rome we are all familiar. Her iron civilization stands clearly photographed. She grasped all that was valuable in the accumulations of her predecessors and massed it in her structure, built of iron founded on granite. At the zenith of her real greatness and power, *eighty-five* per cent. of her population held titles in lands, and cultivated their own. Then her people were happy, prosperous, hardy and brave; her legions were invincible. Then her currency was, in volume, *one thousand eight hundred millions.* When Rome perished, her lands and wealth were in the hands of *two thousand* individuals. Dr. Lord says: 'These two thousand persons owned the world.' Her currency had been contracted by class legislation to less than *two hundred millions.* Allison says: 'The fall of the Roman Empire, so long ascribed to ignorance, slavery, heathenism, and moral corruption, was really brought about by a decline in the gold and silver mines of Spain and Greece.'"

The German historian, from whom we before quoted, says:

"The people gave themselves up in despair in the fields, as beasts of burden lie down beneath their load and refuse to rise. The disintegration of society was almost complete. All public spirit, all generous emotions, all noble aspirations of man shriveled and disappeared as the volume of money shrank, and prices fell. As men decayed, wealth accumulated in the hands of the few. Not only did whole provinces become the property of one man, but usury existed in so frightful a form that even the virtuous Brutus received *sixty* per cent. for the use of money."

Pliny says:

"These colossal fortunes which ruined Italy, were due to *the concentration of estates through usury*, so scarce was money."

This part of the subject might be pursued further, but I will content myself with making one more quotation from Allison.

"Rome," says this great historian, "fell, because the slaves became so numerous, and the proprietors so besotted that none were left to withstand the incursions of the barbarians, except nobles, too effeminate and cowardly to defend their property, and slaves, who had nothing to defend."

This is true. Men will rally to defend their homes and their firesides, while but few are willing to volunteer, or even when drafted, to fight with much earnestness for that which belongs to a master, or for only a bed of straw in a tenement house.

Why did Egypt become decrepit and die? Why did Rome fall? The answer is plain. They both committed suicide by enslaving and killing the masses of their workingmen.

2

The late lamented Col. Heath, in a newspaper article, truthfully and eloquently said:

"Egypt died when *ninety-seven* per cent. of her wealth became centered in *three* per cent. of her population.

"Babylon's fall was caused by *ninety-eight* per cent. of her wealth centering in *two* per cent. of her people.

"Persia, the empire of 'an *hundred and seven and twenty* provinces,' kicked the bucket when *one* per cent. of her population had gobbled up the wealth of the realm.

"Greece, with more tenacity, succumbed to apoplexy when less than *one* per cent. of her wealth was distributed among *ninety-nine* per cent. of her people.

"Rome gave up the ghost when *two thousand* of her nobles owned the world.

"In the American Republic the wealth producers own less than *ten* per cent. of what they have created, and already the Goddess of Liberty begins to show the premonitory symptoms of a fatal congestion."

The above is all true. These things are "an ensample unto us." Shall we examine the wrecks other nations have been compelled to pile up, and avoid the rocks on which they have gone to pieces? As sure as like causes produce like effects, so sure we are in danger. Let us learn by the experience of others.

CHAPTER II.

IN THEIR FOOTSTEPS.

HOW GREED KILLS.—PROPHETS.—LINCOLN'S FEARS.—STE-VEN'S NOTE OF WARNING.—WEBSTER AT BUNKER HILL.—A GREAT COUNTRY.—ENGLISH LANDLORDISM IN AMERICA.—VANDERBILT WORTH MORE THAN ALL CHICAGO.—GEN. WEAVER'S CALCULATION.—OTHER RICH MEN.—STATEMENT FROM KANSAS.—A METHODIST BISHOP ON THE SITUATION.—OUR INDEBTEDNESS AND OUR WEALTH.—TESTIMONIES FROM HERBERT SPENCER, JEFFERSON AND WEBSTER.—JUDGE BLACK'S TESTIMONY—AN OBJECTION AND REPLY.—GEM FROM HENRY GEORGE.

Thus far, our attention has been called to other governments. We have seen how their cupidity has strangled them to death. Avarice generally over-reaches itself and dies from its own hand. If suicide was its first work it would be well, but it is not. Avarice destroys all within its reach before it destroys itself.

In every age of the world there seems to have been here and there a mind which towered above its fellows, as Mount Washington in New Hampshire, or Mount Hermon in Palestine, tower above the little hills by which they are surrounded. Such have seemed gifted with a spirit of prophecy and have

warned their fellow beings of the breakers ahead.
Abraham Lincoln, as the light of the brighter world,
on the border of which he was standing, seemed to
penetrate through the dark clouds of war, raised
his prophetic voice, "as the voice of one crying in the
wilderness," and said:

"Yes, we may all congratulate ourselves that this
cruel war is nearing a close. It has cost a vast amount
of blood and treasure. The best blood of the flower of
American youth has been freely offered upon our country's altar that the nation might live. It has been indeed a trying hour for the Republic; *but I see in the
near future, a crisis approaching that unnerves me,
and causes me to tremble for the safety of my country.
As a result of the war, corporations have been enthroned
and an era of corruption in high places will follow, and
the money power of the country will endeavor to prolong
its reign by working upon the prejudices of the people,
until all wealth is aggregated in a few hands and the
Republic is destroyed. I feel at this moment more anxiety for the safety of my country than ever before, even
in the midst of war. God grant that my suspicions
may prove groundless.*"

Great heavens, what a prophet! How truly did
the then on-coming events cast their shadows on the
far-reaching mind of the man, who, in a few days,
was to fall a martyr to the power which tried to ruin
the country. A more gigantic power just being born
caused him more "anxiety for the safety of his country," than did the war which was waged on purpose
to overthrow it.

This brings to my mind the words of another dying old saint. Thaddeus Stevens, that grand old

commoner from Pennsylvania, after he saw "the hand-writing on the wall," arose from his dying bed, I seem to see him now, as he stands in his place in the congressional chamber, leaning on his cane, hat in hand, and his overcoat over his arm, ready to leave the assembly's hall, and go back to the bed from which he had just arisen on purpose to bear a kind of dying testimony.   His words are:

"There is no great prospect that we shall return to the system I have indicated, nor do much to protect the people from their own eager speculations. When, a few years hence, the people shall have been brought to general bankruptcy by their unregulated enterprise, I shall have the satisfaction to know that I attempted to prevent it."

Eloquent and prophetic words! Yes, honest old Thaddeus, your skirts are clear, you did your duty. Alas! the sheep failed to recognize the voice of the shepherd, and drank to the dregs, the cup prepared by their own "unregulated enterprise."

The people of this country concluded they would erect a granite monument which should tell all future generations of the struggles our fathers had, to give us liberty; they went to Bunker Hill, or rather, Breed's Hill, in Charlestown, Mass., and erected a "granite finger, pointing heavenward." They called upon Massachusetts' great senator, Daniel Webster, to deliver the dedicatory address. In that address he hinted that American liberty was yet in danger, not from foreign foes, but from "foes within." Have we the power to stand against ourselves, was, as it is now, the great question. In that speech, Mr. Webster said:

"Liberty cannot long endure in any country where the tendency of legislation is to concentrate wealth in the hands of a few."

These three texts are not from three "Anarchists," "Communists," or "fire-eaters." They do not come from those who strive to make "labor discontented," and "invested capital uneasy." They are from three of the greatest statesmen the world ever saw. They were old, when the present crisis was forced upon the American people; they are "the voice of one crying in the wilderness," and should be studied—prayerfully studied.

We are in a great country. A New England writer compares our American Republic to a "sleeping giant," whose head lies pillowed on the eternal snows of the North, his feet among the perennial flowers of the South, while, with his left hand he grasps the rising sun, and with his right hand, the setting sun.

We have, in round numbers, *four millions* of square miles of territory, possessing every variety of soil and climate. All the minerals of earth are here; our lakes, rivers and forests are unequaled. One of our *forty* states is larger than England, Scotland, Wales, Belgium, Holland and Portugal. Nearly all Europe could be taken out of Texas. Truly, we have all the latent resources of wealth we could ask. There is enough and to spare. These latent resources are being developed, too, but, "the tendency of legislation is to concentrate the wealth in the hands of a few."

How is it in New York to-day? I have seen the statement that *three* per cent. of the inhabitants of the city, own it; the other *ninety-seven* per cent. are, in a sense, paupers. It is said that less than *one hundred and fifty* men own Ireland. That is a bad state of affairs, but *nineteen* men in England own more land in America than all Ireland; thus British landlordism is destined to be more potent for evil here than in the land of primogenitureship. By these and other means, the wealth of America is passing into the hands of a few men, and some of these men alien landlords. It is said that our William H. Vanderbilt died worth *two hundred and twenty-two millions* of dollars. To get something of an idea of that vast wealth, let it be stated that at that same time, Chicago, with its over half-million of people, had not that much assessable property. Chicago, with all its real estate, all its buildings, all its goods and chattels of all kinds, in the year 1879, I believe, was only assessed at *two hundred and seventeen millions* of dollars. How did Vanderbilt acquire all this wealth? Did he earn it? No; I this day saw a calculation, made by my friend, Gen. Weaver, which showed that if Adam had lived until to-day, and had laid by one dollar every day, he would not yet have one hundred million dollars. That if he had come into existence *six hundred thousand years ago*, instead of six thousand years ago, and laid by one dollar every day, he would not yet have wealth equal to that left by William H. Vanderbilt. Of course, then, it is evident that Vanderbilt did not earn his wealth, but somebody earned it and Vanderbilt got it. People begin to understand this and it occasions much dissatisfaction.

Now, Vanderbilt was only one of the immensely wealthy men of the country; the Goulds, the Scotts, the Garrets, the Huntingtons, the Stanfords, and others were and are rapidly following on, while the millions are becoming poorer every day. May not this great increase of wealth on the part of these men be one cause of the increase of poverty on the part of others? While writing this a Kansas exchange, *Chetopa Statesman*, comes to hand, making the following exhibit of the condition of Labette Co., Kan., as shown by the records of the county:

"Land mortgages............................$6,500,000
Interest past due and unpaid...............   200,000
Railroad and other bonds...................   600,000
Chattel mortgages personal security........   700,000
Unsecured debts............................ 1,000,000

   "Grand Total...............................$9,000,000.

"Leaving out the unsecured debts, the rest of it is drawing interest all the way from 6 to 30 per cent. At a safe estimate, the yearly interest exceeds $700,000.

"This enormous aggregate indebtedness spread over the land of the county (and it ultimately devolves upon the farms to pay all debts) would amount to $300 for every man, woman and child in the county.

"This is certainly a staggering exhibit. It is an appalling fact. And it can neither be forgotten nor pooh-poohed out of the way.

"Under the present financial condition of the country *the payment of this debt is simply and utterly impossible.*

"It is only a question of time when three out of every four mortgages will be foreclosed—when three-fourths of the farmers in this county will be turned out of their homes—unless there is a speedy change in financial legislation."

It is but justice to say that Labette County is no worse off than half the other counties of Kansas. While in Kansas not long since, I was shown the records of Phillips County and partial records of other counties which were quite as startling as the record quoted above.

In the light of the above facts who wonders that the late Methodist Bishop, Dr. Peck, saw the inevitable result, and tearfully said:

"At the beginning the conviction must be profound and pervading that a great reform is imperatively demanded. I take it that the great revolution which has just revealed itself is the concentration of the general feeling that in some way *reform must come.* Agitation and conflict are inevitable! This is no child's play! It will be the attempt of moral principles to assault and break down the power of untold consolidated millions of money, to challenge and defy the most enormous class interests, which ever trampled upon a free people. *It will be the most terrific conflict ever known on this continent.*"

This man has hit the case exactly; the battle is to be one between moral principle on the one hand and consolidated millions on the other. If principles gain in this conflict, the sun of our Republic is just beginning to rise; if consolidated and corporate wealth gain this battle, then, indeed, our end has come; greed will choke itself to death.

Our National, State, Municipal, Corporate, and Individual debts to-day, have been estimated to amount to *sixteen thousand million dollars.* One man, a member of Congress, said on the floor of the House, they were over *twenty thousand millions.* The interest will average as much as six per cent. The total increase of wealth in the country is not over three and a half per cent. Now add three and a half per cent. on *forty-five thousand millions* the county is receiving, and deduct six per cent. on *twenty thousand millions* we are paying and you will readily determine how much there will be left with which to feed, clothe and provide homes for *sixty millions* of people. This represents our Republic as a Republic of paupers on the one hand and of robbers on the other. Such a Republic cannot stand. Herbert Spencer rightly said:

"The republican form of government is the highest form, but, because of this, it requires the highest type of human nature—a type no where at present existing. We have not grown up to it, nor have you."

I fear Mr. Spencer is correct, especially in that

last sentence. "*We* [Englishmen] *have not grown up to it, nor have you* [Americans].

Thomas Jefferson regarded the people, the "common people," as being all right; he feared the wealthy classes only. He said:

"I am not among those who fear the people; they and not the rich are our dependence for continued freedom."

Daniel Webster told us:

"The great interest of this country—the producing cause of its prosperity is labor! *labor!* LABOR! The government was made to encourage and protect this industry and to give it security."

Has the government done, and is it doing what Massachusetts' great statesman said it was organized to do? Let the late Judge Black answer the question.

"The actual consequences resulting to the country from the measures of the monopolists, have not, I think, been truly represented, or properly considered. *For many years all legislation has been partial to capitalists*, and correspondingly injurious to the rights of land and labor. To what pernicious extent this system has been carried I need not say, for it is seen and known of all men. It cannot and will not come to good. * * * But for every millionaire, they have made a thousand paupers. The relations between workingmen and employers have never been so unsatisfactory as now. Laborers are complaining everywhere of inadequate wages; and the complaint is true, without doubt. The law ought to secure them a living rate of compensation; but capital has got labor by the throat, and will not suffer anything done for its relief. * * * If we estimate the prosperity of a country only by the overgrown fortunes of individuals especially favored by law, then

Ireland is prosperous, as well as America; for there, as here, the legal machinery is in perfect order, which makes the rich richer, while it grinds the poor down to deeper poverty; and there, as here, the lines of Gold-Smith are ever true and ever wise:

'Hard fares the state, to hastening ills a prey,
Where wealth accumulates and men decay.'"

It is objected that the state of affairs hinted at in the foregoing cannot obtain in America. I remember of delivering a lecture on these subjects; at its close a gentleman came to me and said: "Mr. Hull, you make out a case, but then it is all in your eye; great fortunes may be made in America in a single life-time; but it is only for a life-time; what the father makes and hordes up the sons will scatter. To bring about the state of things you fear, we must have the laws of entail, of primogeniture-ship, and must have dukedoms, baronies and lord-ships. Those never can obtain in America."

Were it not for the fact that this man was ostensibly wrong, at first sight one might incline to think he was correct. Upon second thought one can see that all these wants are supplied under one word, and that is *corporation*. Corporations which never die and consequently need no heirs, have more than taken the place of lords, dukes, earls and barons of the old countries.

Coal and water, to-day provides physical force with which muscles of flesh cannot compete; thus, labor becomes a "drug in the market." The never-dying corporation harnesses the steam horse to his machinery, and uses the lightning as his errand boys. The store-houses of nature are tapped and their goods are forced into the market. Who can compete with them? These dukes and barons own about all the surplus land of America, and the "children" whose "bread" was wrongfully given to and retained by these "dogs," are forced to starve in the streets.

These institutions, known as corporations, are a new class of individuals, a class not known in our constitution; but this individual is possessed of a thousand times the greed and avarice of any foreign lord. Unless our Constitution is remodeled so as to take this *person* in and make him subject to the people, he will soon scuttle that document and overthrow American civilization.

Can we bring this new person, monopoly, to terms? Can we make him one of us? Can we instil into him the elements of brotherhood? If so, we have indeed a glorious future. Poverty would be abolished, want would be destroyed and glorious achievements accomplished. Henry George pictures the state of affairs which would then ensue, as follows:

"With want destroyed; with greed changed to noble passions; with the fraternity that is born of equality taking the place of jealousy and fear that array men against each other; with mental power loosened by conditions that gives to the humblest, comfort and leisure and who shall measure the heights to which our civilization may soar? Words fail the thought! It is the golden age of which poets have sung and high-raised seers have told in metaphor. It is the glorious vision which has always haunted man with gleams of fitful splendor."

How grand the idea above expressed! and who shall say it is more grand than true? Remove poverty and the fear of poverty, and avarice is forever gone. Greed then will no longer drive men to robbery and theft. The life of the higher faculties will then be called into play, and

"Sword and spear of needless worth
Shall prune the tree and plow the earth."

CHAPTER III.

DO THE PEOPLE RULE?

IGNORANCE THE BANE OF REPUBLICS.—STUPIDITY AND CUPID-
ITY SHOULD BE DISFRANCHISED.—BULLDOZING.—A MO-
NOPOLIST'S SPEECH.—THE EFFECT.—ADVICE FROM THE
BOSTON HERALD.—HOW ELECTIONS ARE CONDUCTED IN
PHILADELPHIA AND NEW YORK.—ONE OF THE RIDDLES TO
BE SOLVED.—A SENATOR ON THE QUESTION.—WHAT THE
WALLACE COMMITTEE FOUND.—LAW OF RHODE ISLAND.—
COL. MORAN'S TESTIMONY.—DANIEL O'DONOVAN TESTI-
FIES.—ELOQUENT WORDS FROM HON. F. O. WILLEY.—AN
EX-MEMBER OF CONGRESS DISFRANCHISED.—COMMITTEE'S
GLOOMY REPORT.—SHALL WE GIVE UP SO?

Abraham Lincoln defined a Republic to be a government of the people, for the people, and by the
people. In this he was right; nothing less can be
called democratic republicanism. With intelligence and integrity to guarantee such a government,
Republics are demanded and are the only true form
of government, but without both intelligence and
integrity we had better be under a czar in Russia,
or a sultan in Turkey than in a Republic. A republican form of government can only be good in
the hands of honest and wise citizens. Ignorance
blindfolds the voters and is as liable to lead to hell,

as anywhere; and a lack of integrity will lead the voter and drive the government in any direction demagogues may point. Once a gentleman remarked to me, after hearing me talk: "You are right, but I never should vote that way; when I go to the polls I go there to win, and your theories never can win." Why not? because men either lack intelligence to comprehend the truth, or, comprehending it, lack the honor to go to the polls and express their own opinions. In either case, such people should be disfranchised; why should stupidity or cupidity be privileged to vote away the liberties of *sixty millions* of people? If such people had only their own destiny in their hands, it would be but little matter; but in this country all are, unfortunately, in the hands of knaves and imbeciles, provided they are in the majority.

But with all the wisdom and honor in the world, things are so manipulated here that the people cannot rule. Bulldozing, as it is called, is almost the rule, and not the exception. Where there is a law against bulldozing, those who seek to control the elections always find a way to violate it without being held guilty. I remember, in the year 1878, I think it was, when General Butler was running for Governor of Massachusetts, one of the proprietors of cotton mills at Holyoke, called his hands together on Friday afternoon before the election on the next Tuesday, and spoke, in substance, as follows:

"Next Tuesday is election; your employers would not, if they could, dictate how any of you shall vote; we want you to go to the polls, if you choose, and vote *as you* choose; but, this corporation has concluded, if the present party continues in power, to continue to run these mills, and do all it can for those in its employ; but if General Butler is elected, we have concluded to shut down, and not a spindle shall turn while he is Governor of this State. His administration will so disturb the relation of things as they now exist, that we will do no business as long as he is governor."

This came to me at first hand, from a member who was called in to hear that speech. Said he, fully three-fourths of us had made up our minds to vote for Butler, but when we found we were voting ourselves out of employment, and voting bread out of our children's mouths—when we realized that a long and cold winter was just ahead of us, we saw that it would not do. Two out of about three hundred of us were rash enough to vote for Butler and take our chances as to the result. The rest argued, we will, if we vote for Butler, elect him or we will not; if we elect him, we have voted ourselves out of employment; if we do not our vote has done no good; the result was, they either stayed at home or voted for the opposition candidate.

3

This was a kind of bulldozing that the law could not touch, still it was effectual. In such cases the question at the head of this chapter is *a propos. Do the people rule?*

The above mentioned firm and a thousand others in the Old Bay State, may have taken their *cue* from an editorial in the *Boston Herald*, of which the following is an extract:

"They [the capitalists] know that idle hands are waiting to do their work. It is not to be expected that they will look on indifferently, and see their employers vote for a destructive like Butler. Human nature is much the same in Massachusetts and Mississippi, only methods are different. Brain, capital and enterprise will tell in any community. It is very improper, of course, to intimidate voters. But there is a way of giving advice that is quite convincing."

The North, on the eve of every general election, hears much about bulldozing in the South; the South probably hears as much about it in the North; if not, it is simply because it is slow in gathering facts. The story of elections in Philadelphia and New York is told in the respective papers of these cities plainly enough to open the eyes of those who are verdant enough to think the people have some voice in governmental affairs. The history of elections in Cincinnati, and in Chicago, if written true to the facts in the case, would be on a par with the cities mentioned in the following extracts. The first is from the *Public Ledger*, a republican paper of the republican city of Philadelphia. Here it is, slightly abridged:

"The whole fabric of Philadelphia election affairs *is permeated and undermined by fraud.* * * * It [the election] begins with myths on the registry lists; it is carried on by hired gangs of 'rounders,' 'repeaters' and 'personators' who vote, not only for false names on the lists, but the true names of persons who have died, moved away, or are absent from home. *They even vote the names of persons who are at home, and who, on reaching the polls, find themselves shut out."*

The *New York Post* quotes the above, and comments on it as follows:

"Rascality knows no political distinctions. A knave will as readily assume republican as democratic patriotism. * * * New York has been governed by a democratic machine, Philadelphia has been governed by a republican machine. There is no working difference between the two machines."

Comment seems needless; our government is to-day in the hands of a gang of pirates, who, if they cannot run it in their own interest, will attempt to scuttle it. One of the riddles propounded by the American Sphinx to-day is: How can you rescue your so-called Republic from the hands of the Shylocks and the political prostitutes—professional politicians —and deliver it into the hands of the people? The life of republicanism and of civilization in America depends on our ability to solve that among other problems.

A United States Senator has been lauded to the skies for saying:

"We need a stronger government; the *wealth* of the country demands it. * * * The wealth of the country has to bear the burdens of the government *and shall control it.*"

This is the principle now almost universally acted upon. The Wallace Committee, appointed in 1879, to investigate bulldozing in the United States, found the rich bullying the poor into voting their tickets, not only in the South, but in all the New England States; in New York, New Jersey, Pennsylvania, Ohio and Indiana. They found on the statute books of Rhode Island, a law from which the following is an abridged extract:

"The following classes of persons have a right * * * to vote in the election of all civil officers, and on all questions, in all legally organized town, ward or district meetings. Every native male citizen, * * * who shall show by legal proof that he has * * * paid a tax upon his property, in the town where he shall offer to vote, *valued at least at one hundred and thirty-four dollars.*

"Second. Every male citizen * * * who is truly and really possessed in his own right, of real estate in such town or city, *of the value of one hundred dollars, over and above all incumbrances,* or which shall rent for *seven dollars per annum* over and above any rent reserved or the interest on any incumbrance thereon."

Under this law the poor man in Rhode Island is effectually disfranchised. Senator Sharon could, in this State, at least, realize his determination that "capital shall control the government." The Wallace Committee took many testimonies on the working of this law in Rhode Island.

The following is an abridgment of Col. James Moran's testimony:

"Live here—lived here twenty-eight years. * * * Entered the service of the United States from Rhode Island. * * * Held an election for officials in Rhode Island in his company, in the army, but could not vote himself. Was a voter once, because he once owned real estate; has lost it and cannot vote now."

This poor fellow was good enough to go and fight to save his country, but could not vote for its officers—that privilege, in his State, belongs to the real estate owners.

Daniel O'Donovan testified before the Committee as follows:

"Ten of us work together in one room in our factory; the highest grade room in it; six of the ten cannot vote for want of land."

On this point, Hon. F. O. Willey, to whom I am indebted for many extracts in this chapter, says:

"The mechanics of Rhode Island have woven some of the finest fabrics that beautify the ladies' toilet; they clothe her millionaires in fine raiment; they have decked her hills with palaces, in which their masters walk on velvet carpets, and sleep on beds of down; they have cleft granite from her quarries and filled her valleys with factories and made them vocal with the hum of industry; they have pierced her hills, and sent the engine whizzing through her mountains and across her fields; they have built her temples of worship and her ships that sail the sea, yea, and spun the cable that spans old ocean. Yet, unless they happen to own land they cannot vote; they have created her wealth and built up her material prosperity, but must leave it to others to control her political destiny."

The testimony of Hon. Thomas Davis is as important as any yet presented. Here it is:

"Live in Providence; * * * seventy-five years old;
a manufacturing jeweler; been in both branches of the
Legislature a number of times; member of Congress
from Rhode Island in 1853-4, then owned real estate; *I
am not now a qualified voter;* I failed in business,
and the title of my property passed to my assignees,
and I cannot now vote; wealth controls suffrage in
Rhode Island; money is all-powerful here—it can over-
whelm public sentiment at any time here; have been
both a Republican and a Democrat, but have always
advocated the repeal of the restriction."

I might follow this with other evidence until the
heart would grow sick, but I will not; suffice it,
that the Wallace Committee found legal and illegal
restrictions in *every State visited.* The most humiliating part of the whole is that they were compelled to report to the Senate as follows:

"Your committee was instructed to inquire and report whether it is within the competency of Congress
to provide by additional legislation for the more perfect right of suffrage to citizens of the United States in
all the States of the Union. They have performed that
duty, and whilst they find that improper practices, as
herein before detailed, exist in the States visited, and
the freedom of choice by voters in those States has been
interfered with and persons practically threatened with
dismissal from employment, if they voted in opposition
to the wishes of their employers, *yet they cannot find
that it is within the competency of Congress to correct
this wrong by additional or any legislation.*"

This settles the question; if this committee is
right in its report, the people do not rule. Our
liberties are at an end. The question of our own

Sphinx cannot be answered, and our civilization must die. How the hearts of those who have boasted of our civilization must sink when they contemplate the fact that our republican institutions have produced giant enemies of republicanism too strong for congressional legislation to control!

We are not willing to give it up so; we believe there is virtue yet with the people. Still other dangers threaten us, which must be considered in after chapters, after which we hope to be able to point the way out.

CHAPTER IV.

WHAT IS THE PRESS DOING?

JESUS' CHARGE AGAINST LAWYERS.—WHY THE JEWS LOST THEIR
POLITY.—THE POWER OF THE PRESS.—PRESS AND PULPIT
CONTRASTED.—IMPORTANCE OF INTEGRITY.—HOW THE
PRESS MURDERED FOUR MEN.—A "BOSTON HERALD" RE-
PORT.—IT RELUCTANTLY MAKES A CORRECTION.—MR.
THURBER'S TESTIMONY.—SENATOR WINDOM ON THE QUES-
TION.—SCATHING REBUKE FROM A JOURNALIST.

Of all the charges that Jesus made against the
pharisees, and particularly the lawyers of his time,
probably the most heinous one was that made in
Luke xi:52, that they had "taken away the key of
knowledge." The pharisees, to whom this charge
in Matt. xxiii, applies, pretended to be the especial
conservators of knowledge; and the lawyers, to
whom the charge applies in Luke, xi, had been educated by especial provision, on purpose to read
and expound the law to the multitude. The multitude was compelled to go from Sabbath to Sabbath
on purpose to listen and thus learn what the law was.

It appears that these pharisaic lawyers took advantage of the occasion to make their position con-

tribute to the ignorance instead of the knowledge of the multitude. They gave the multitude what they chose to have them know, and nothing more. Thus, they were just what Jesus calls them; "blind guides"—"blind leaders of the blind" into the ditch. The Jews lost their polity through the wilful ignorance and perversity of their lawyers.

Jesus foresaw the state of affairs their course would bring, hence he said:

"Woe unto you, ye lawyers! for ye have taken away the key of knowledge; ye entered not in yourselves, and them that were entering ye hindered."

The daily and weekly newspaper has, in this country become the great educator of the people. The pulpit has largely lost its power; not half, in our large cities—not one-fifth of the people go to church; the minister, if he would, cannot reach them. Again, if he could reach them, he only has access to their ears an hour at a time once a week; but the omnipresent and ubiquitous newspaper penetrates all the dark corners of our Republic and provides the theme and gives direction to the thought of the civilized world. This being true, press and type have become the lever and fulcrum which moves the world of thought.

The world is indebted to the press to-day for much of its knowledge, and for the most of its future progress; how important then that intelligence and integrity be placed at its helm. When the press neglects its duty, or when, through misrepresentation and falsehood, it gives impetus to the wrong set of thoughts, or sets men to thinking in the wrong direction, it not only takes away the key of knowledge, but becomes an immense engine to force falsehood, and consequent destruction to the front.

Two cases occur to my mind now, which serve to illustrate my point. In the trial of the four men recently murdered in Chicago, under the guise of law, there is no doubt in the world but the newspapers, in obedience to monopolistic capitalists, committed the murder. They worked up public sentiment, so that as the high priest, Caiaphas, said:

"It is expedient for us that one man [seven men should die for the people."

In that trial, newspaper reporters swore that they went to anarchistic meetings under instructions to make their reports as unfavorable to the anarchists as possible, thus to create a sentiment against them that would lead to murder. This would please the capitalists and give the newspapers a much larger sale.

A labor reform convention was once held in the city of Boston, which I did not attend. The *Boston Herald* reported that the profane and blasphemous Moses Hull was there, and in his speech uttered such profanities and vulgarities as would have driven a decent audience out of the hall. In its report of the evening session, it said: "At this time Moses Hull again took the stand and proceeded to swear and blackguard the audience out of the hall."

I went to the *Herald* and told it there must be some mistake in the matter, as I had not been at the convention. The city editor responded: "Well, as you are a very profane man, you are not much injured if the report is not true." I said: "As I never swore an oath in my life, I am injured; I ask you to take back what you have said, and if you do not, I will try my hand in a libel suit." He said: "It shall be taken back, Mr. Hull." The next day the paper said:

"Moses Hull called at the *Herald* office yesterday, and requests us to say that he did not swear as much in the recent labor convention as our report represented."

I went back to the office and said: "You have lied again. Once more I ask you to take it back— to state that I was not at the convention; that I am not a blackguard nor a profane man. I will not call again. The next time you hear from me it will be through General Butler." The next day the *Herald* said:

"The *Herald* reporter was mistaken. Moses Hull did not attend the convention where he was represented as swearing profanely. The swearing was done by—— ——,who can swear enough for a whole labor reform convention."

The *Herald* boasted of a circulation of about *ninety-seven thousand;* see what a power for mischief when misdirected. It may not be out of place for me to say here, this was the last attempt of the *Boston Herald* to slander me.

Mr. Thurber, president of the Anti-Monopoly League, writes as follows:

"On the twenty-seventh day of January, 1880, Mr. Franklin B. Gowen, president of the Philadelphia and Reading Railroad, in an argument before the Committee on Commerce of the House of Representatives of the United States, in Washington, stated:

'I have heard the counsel of the Pennsylvania Railroad Company, standing in the Supreme Court of Pennsylvania, threaten that court with the displeasure of his clients if it decided against them, and all the blood in my body tingled with shame at the humiliating spectacle.'

In the Associated Press reports this was suppressed, and only when the argument was published by Mr. Gowen was this remarkable statement verified to those who heard it."

This shows how totally the Associated Press is in the hands of railroad and other corporations. They simply give to the world that portion of the news they want it to have—no more. Is this fair? Is it honest? Can the world be truly enlightened by such a press? I fear not.

When I took my pen to write this chapter I had only one thing in my mind; that was to reply to the question so frequently asked: "If what you have stated concerning bulldozing and preventing people from expressing their honest opinions at the polls is true, why have we heard so little of it?

Why does the press say nothing? To this there is but one answer; the press is subsidized, controlled almost wholly by the monopolistic, bulldozing corporations, and therefore either says nothing, or seeks to whitewash such operations.

Senator Windom, of Minnesota, in a letter to the Anti-Monopoly League, said:

"The capitalists have bought and are buying largely the Associated Press, and are controlling largely the avenues of intelligence."

Could I bring the matter within the limits allotted to this chapter, I could bring a hundred illustrative cases bearing on this point.

I repeat, the press of America has become the toadying tool of monopolists, and should we lose our republicanism and our civilization, the press, which could, if it would, enlighten the public, will be largely to blame.

Once upon a time the press got up an annual excursion; when it reached New York, a great dinner was provided for it. At this feast a leading New York journalist was called upon to respond to the toast, "The Independent Press." For a long time he refused to speak, but after much persuasion, and observing that he was talking to and for the press, and not for the world, he said:

"There is no such thing in America as an independent press, unless it is out in the country towns. *You are all slaves.* You know it and I know it. There is

not one of you who dares to express an honest opinion.
If you express it, you would know before hand that it
would never appear in print.   I am paid *one hundred
and fifty dollars* for keeping honest opinions out of the
paper I am connected with.   Others of you are paid
similar salaries for doing similar things.   If I should
allow honest opinions to be printed in one issue of my
paper, like Othello, before twenty-four hours my occu-
pation would be gone.   The man who would be so foolish as to write honest opinions would be out on the
street hunting for another job.   The business of a New
York journalist *is to distort the truth, to lie outright,
to pervert, to vilify, to fawn at the feet of mammon,
and to sell his country and his race for his daily bread,*
or for what is about the same thing, his salary.   You
know this and I know it; and what foolery to be toast-
ing an "Independent Press."   We are the tools and
the vassals of rich men behind the scenes.   We are
jumping-jacks.   They pull the string and we dance.
Our time, our talents, our lives, our possibilities, are all
the property of other men.   *We are intellectual prostitutes.*"

Great heavens!   What an arraignment! and the
worst feature of it is, the most severe things here
said are true.   The press, which could save the country, is leading the way to the city of destruction.

CHAPTER V.

DANGER SIGNALS.

DESIGNS OF CAPITALISTS AND CORPORATIONS.—THE MODUS OPERANDI OF MAKING A NATION OF TASK MASTERS AND SERFS.—WORK OF THE EVANGELICAL ALLIANCE.—A LATE SENATOR'S POSITION.—WHAT THE PRESS HAS SAID.—DANGER SIGNAL HOISTED BY PRESIDENT LINCOLN.—"THE DICTATOR" AND "THE IMPERIALIST."—AN EDITOR'S TESTIMONY.—INTENTIONS OF A PROMINENT CANDIDATE FOR THE PRESIDENCY.—QUEEN VICTORIA'S OPINION OF GRANT.—A PRESIDENT FAVORS THE BRITISH SYSTEM.—LET US PUT A LOOKOUT ALOFT.

It is the evident design of capitalists and corporations to bring our Republic to an end. It is hard to control the multitude so long as they have a vote; but deprive them of their right to express an opinion at the ballot box and the country is then in the hands of corporations; laboring men become at once a race of plebeians and will soon be relegated to a position analagous to that occupied by the slaves of a former generation.

It could hardly be expected that the first move in this direction would be to urge that a republican form of government must come to an end. That would be disfranchising the whole nation at once;

47

the first move will be to make certain ones help to
take the rights of citizens from the balance; when
the example has been set by disfranchising one class,
that can be pointed to as a precedent and the task
of making this a nation of task-masters on one hand
and of serfs on the other will be comparatively easy.

A convention of the Evangelical Alliance in Washington, D. C., Dec. 8, 1887, urged that the common
laborer must be disfranchised and others prevented
from landing in this country.   Let that succeed and
the next move will be to disfranchise the mechanic;
next, the liberties of the farmer will go, and so on
until America becomes a paradise of millionaires
and a slave-pen of paupers.

The late Senator Sharon in urging that "the
wealth of the country has to bear the burdens of
government, and it should control it," only meant
the disfranchisement of the poor—nothing less.
He said:

"The people are being educated up to this theory
rapidly, and the sooner this theory is recognized in the
constitution and laws, the better it will be for the people."

Of course he foresaw that such a revolution could
not be precipitated all at once without an immense
flow of blood, and said:

"Without bloodshed, and rivers of it, there will be
no political change of administration. * * * To
avert bloodshed a strong central government should
be established as soon as possible."

The Indianapolis *Daily Journal* argued in the same strain. It said:

"There is too much freedom in this country, rather than too little."

The *Daily News*, of the same city, said:

"If the workingmen had no vote, they would be more amenable to the teachings of the hard times."

The *Richmond* (*Va.*,) *State*, stated the matter more plainly. Its words are:

"There are defects in our institutions which can only be remedied by irregular means, and the most defective portion of the machinery of our government is the elective. The best [that means the most wealthy] must govern in every State, and will, regardless of any attempt to deprive them of that right."

Though President Lincoln's warning has been used in a previous chapter, I dare not leave it out here; it serves as a kind of a text for a sermon. In his first message to Congress he said:

"Monarchy is sometimes hinted at as a possible refuge from the power of the people. In my present position I would be scarcely justified were I to omit exercising a warning voice against returning despotism. There is one point to which I ask attention; it is the effort to place capital on an equal footing with, if not above labor, in the structure of the government. I bid the laboring people beware of surrendering a power which they already possess, and which, when surrendered, will surely be used to close the door of advancement to such as they, and fix new disabilities and burdens upon them till all of liberty shall be lost."

This was written before many of the huge monopolies which now crush the life out of the people, were born; yet this grand man, with prophetic eye, looked forward and seemed to see the very movement which now threatens the life of the American Republic. He bids us *"beware."* Of what? *"Returning despotism!"* How will it be brought about? By the *"placing of capital above labor in the structure of the government.* Heaven help us to heed this warning before it is too late.

In 1877-8 I had two exchanges on my list advocating that republicanism had proved a failure and must be superceded by something else; one was called *The Imperialist;* the other, *The Dictator.* I was astonished, as I passed these papers to callers in my office, to hear the general sympathy there was expressed with the sentiments of these papers.

Whitelaw Reid said in 1874, in the *New York Tribune:*

"It is astonishing, yea, startling, the extent to which the faith prevails, in money circles in New York, that we ought to have a monarchy."

Since Jay Gould has a deed of Whitelaw Reid, and owns the *New York Tribune,* probably it will never express astonishment again at the general opinion that we ought to have a monarchy.

There is little doubt but that could Gen. Grant have received the nomination and election for the third term of the presidency, his inauguration would have sounded the tocsin, and liberty, before his four years' term would have expired, would have been at an end. He had been East studying the monarchies of the Old World. Behind this long sojourn among the monarchies of the Old World lay a motive not apprehended by the multitude. When the national convention which it was supposed would have nominated Grant for a third term was over, and Garfield, instead of Grant was nominated, the Associated Press brought the news that:

"Queen Victoria is very fond of General Grant and is disappointed that he is not nominated."

The Queen had the description of Grant's tour around the world, especially bound for her at an expense of $40,00 per set.

Mr. Willey supposes the General did not win the Queen by arguments in behalf of American democracy—that her fondness for him rather grew out of his toadying to her monarchical ideas.

President Arthur, in his first message to Congress argued that the British system of office-holding should be adopted in this country—that "the tenure of office should be for life," and adds:

"That this system as an entirety has proved very successful in Great Britain seems to be generally conceded even by those who once opposed its adoption. *To a statute which should incorporate its general features, I should feel bound to give my approval.*"

Thus it is demonstrated that we had a president,

lately who was ready to hand this government over as a monarchy if only Congress had asked him to do so. I do not say this to speak against the late president, for I doubt whether a more honorable man has occupied the presidential chair since Abraham Lincoln. I present it simply as a danger signal. There are breakers ahead! If republicanism is to be preserved it will be by vigilant watching, and a continual lifting up of voices of warning. The plans of capitalists and corporations must be known by the masses, and checkmated at the polls. Let us be vigilant.

CHAPTER VI.

DO MONOPOLIES CONTROL GOVERNMENT?

HOW THE GOVERNMENT SURRENDERED TO THE BANKS.—WHAT THE MONEY POWER ASKED AND GOT.—OUR BONDED DEBT NOT CAUSED BY THE WAR.—WHAT CHARTERS DO.—CONTRARY TO THE DECLARATION OF INDEPENDENCE.—HOW CORPORATIONS MONOPOLIZE EVERYTHING.—RAILROADS STRONGER THAN CONGRESS.—TESTIMONY OF A SENATE COMMITTEE.—APATHY, OUR CHIEF DANGER.—GOWEN'S TESTIMONY.—COURTS THREATENED.—JAY GOULD'S TESTIMONY.—CAPITALISTIC SECRET SOCIETIES.—GOULD, ALL THINGS TO ALL MEN.—SENATOR DAVIS' TESTIMONY.—RAILROADS BRIBING A LEGISLATURE.—ELOQUENT WORDS FROM HON. F. O. WILLEY.

In Republics the people rule. I shall now show that in this country the people are ruled by the wealthy classes, especially by those possessing incorporated wealth. The facts which occurred in 1879 and 1880 are sufficient to show our government entirely under the money power. When the bill was up to recharter the National Banks, the banks threatened, that if they were not rechartered, they would create such a panic as this country never saw; the result was, President Hayes hauled the stars and stripes down from the masthead and asked the bankers what they wanted, and promised it to them. The first thing President Garfield did, when he became chief magistrate, a few days after, was to run up the white flag; he promised the bankers that no legislation in this country would receive his sanction, which did not suit them. The banks must stand though the government falls.

The money corporations asked the government for the bonds, and got them. They asked for the bonds to be put on sale at *market* value, instead of *par* value, and got it: they asked that the interest on the bonds be paid in coin, instead of lawful money, and got it; they asked that the bonds be freed from taxes, and they got it; they asked that the bonds be taken back and in their stead new ones be issued, *principal and interest* payable in coin, and they got that. All these legislations were squarely against the people and in favor of money monopolists. Is that republicanism? Does not this look as though a single monopoly was controling an entire department of the government?

It is generally supposed that our bonded debt was created by the war and was to help us out with the war, but such was not the case. The war could have been fought and every cent of the expense paid as we went along without creating any debt. The bonds and the banks have cost us more and been more disastrous to us, as a people, than the war.

The *Chicago Express*, after tabulating all the expenses of the war and of the bonds, says:

"According to this statement, the pay, cost of food and clothing of the volunteers amounted to $1,767,064-130, while the bondholders to the date of June 30th, 1879, was $1,764,246,198, and another year's interest must be added to find the amount paid to the present date. Thus we find that the bondholders were paid over fifty millions more for their services than the soldiers were paid for theirs. Not only this, but the bondholders are to receive back double their principle invested—a principle which was loaned in depreciated currency to be paid back in gold or its equivalent. The soldier's principle of health, of strength, of vigorous constitution is gone forever, and can never be repaid."

In another chapter this subject will come up again. For the present I pass more directly to the subject hinted at in the heading.

Before showing how corporations are attempting to run this government it may not be out of place to say a few words on corporations in general. Those who think charters give people rights or even confer privileges on the corporate bodies are mistaken; that is not their object, their object is to take rights from all others. I have a natural right to build a railroad where I please, provided I purchase the right of way of those who own the land through which my road runs, and pay all other damages caused by my road. A charter does not grant me that privilege, it only acts as a prohibition against others; my charter deprives you of the right to build a road along by the side of mine; thus it makes a monopoly of my road.

The charter itself, is contrary to the spirit of the

Declaration of Independence. Its language is: "We hold these truths to be self-evident, that all men are created *equal*." Is there equality in investing one with a legal right to do a piece of work and depriving another of the same right?

The object of incorporating is to give advantage to those incorporated. Surely, if no advantage is to be gained by incorporating there would be no corporations. These corporations not only monopolize the privileges supposed to be granted, and, in reality, take from others, but they monopolize the best of everything else. They always aim to have in their employ the best business men, the best lawyers, the best editors and the best inventors the country can produce; they cannot afford to ignore talent in any direction, and they intend to make it hot for the talent that ignores them. A writer says:

"In attracting to themselves the service of the most active and vigorous intellects and strongest wills the confederate monopolies are doubly entrenched. The past history of the world gives no system of oppression so insidious, so strong and so all-pervading as that of the predatory corporations which are absorbing the substance and undermining the liberties of the American people."

The above is sufficient to show the power, in any given direction, of these corporations. They have a monopoly on about all the purchasable talent in the country, what is the result? Why, the railroads are stronger than Congress—the fact is they own Congress and they own the commissioners. Vanderbilt declared it would be impossible to appoint commissioners who would not either own the railroads or the railroads would own them.

Of course if they owned the railroads they would work for their own interest; if the railroads owned them they would be manipulated by the roads which owned them.

In 1874, the Senate appointed an especial committee on transportation, of which William Windom, of Minnesota, was chairman. In its report, that committee said:

"In the matter of taxation there are to-day four men, representing the four great trunk lines between Chicago and New York, *who possess, and who, not unfrequently exercise powers which the Congress of the United States would not venture to exert.* They may at any time, and for any reason satisfactory to themselves, by a single stroke of the pen, reduce the value of property in this country by hundreds of millions of dollars. An additional charge of five cents per bushel, on the transportation of cereals, would have been equivalent to a tax of *forty-five millions* of dollars on the crop of 1873. No Congress would dare to exercise so vast a power except upon a necessity of the most imperative nature, and yet, these gentlemen exercise it whenever it suits their supreme will and pleasure, without explanation or apology."

Just think of one sentence in the above. *"Four men * * * can, by a single stroke of the pen, reduce the value of property in this country by many hundreds of millions of dollars."* And this statement does not come from a bevy of cranks, but from a committee of the United States Senate, selected by that body on purpose to gather facts on the subject. Does this look as though the country was in the hands of monopolists, or does it not?

More to be dreaded than anything else is the nation's apathy. Surely here is the place to "cry aloud and spare not," but instead of "lifting up their voices like trumpets," and showing the people their sins, they ostracise, vilify and slander those whose eyes are open to see the approaching danger. "O Lord, open this man's eyes that he may see!"

In a former chapter, in showing up the fact that the press was in the hands of rich corporations, I quoted Mr. Frank Gowen's testimony. I now reproduce that evidence to show the hold these corporations have on the courts. Mr. Thurber presents the testimony as follows:

"On the twenty-seventh day of January, 1880, Mr. Franklin B. Gowen, president of the Philadelphia & Reading Railroad, in an argument before the Committee on Commerce of the House of Representatives of the United States, in Washington, stated:

'I have heard the counsel of the Pennsylvania Railroad Company, standing in the Supreme Court of Pennsylvania, threaten that court with the displeasure of his clients, if it decides against them, and all the blood in my body tingles with shame at the humiliating spectacle.'

In the Associated Press reports this was suppressed, and only when the argument was published by Mr. Gowen, was this remarkable statement verified to those who heard it."

It has long been known by those who have investigated the question, that the legislative department of the government was almost hopelessly in the hands of corporations; but, never before was the Supreme Court of a sovereign State so bulldozed by corporations, through their attorneys. Our Supreme Courts are selected from men of the most profound learning,—men, if any can be found, entirely above suspicion, yet when the counsel of a great corporation goes before that body, he makes a threat which implies that, like the lower courts, legislatures and monopolies, the highest tribunal in the land must strive not to gain the displeasure of his clients.

Does that or does it not show a disposition on the part of corporations to rule this country? When the law-making and the law-executing power of this country is in their hands where are our liberties—where is our republicanism?

Mr. Thurber proves beyond the possibility of dispute, that it had been the custom of the Erie railroad to control elections by bulldozing voters, and by paying, sometimes, more than a million dollars per year out of its treasury.

Jay Gould, the president of the company, was one of the witnesses examined; his testimony, according to Mr. Thurber's quotations from Watson's testimonies, was, that:

"He could distinctly recall that he had been in the habit of sending money into the numerous districts all over the State, either to control nominations or elections for Senators, and Members of the Assembly; considered as a rule, such investments paid better than to wait till men got to Albany, he added the significant remark, upon being asked a question, that it would be as impossible to specify the numerous instances as it would to recall the numerous freight cars sent over the road from day to day."

The report, of which the above is an extract, has opened many eyes. Investigations have sprung up in other quarters and the result is there is an abundance of proof that the Erie railroad is not the only one that buys its friends into office. I have the proof direct from a member of the last Kansas legislature, that the Santa Fe railroad, elected, directly or indirectly, every man it felt it needed in the last Legislature.

This gentleman told me that, to his knowledge, there was a secret order at work among capitalists, the very existence of which there was an effort to keep as a profound secret. The object of this order is to control nominations, where necessary, in all parties, and always to control elections in the successful party. That the conventions in the political parties are manipulated by monopolists through this secret party, without the members of the convention themselves knowing anything of the power behind the throne. Thus we are driven up and voted by the grasping monopolists.

I must return to Mr. Gould's testimony before this committee. He said:

"I do not know how much I paid towards helping friendly men. We had four States to look after, and *we had to suit our politics to circumstances.* In a *Democratic district I was a Democrat; in a Republican district I was a Republican,* and in a doubtful district I was doubtful; but in every district, and at all times I have been an Erie railroad man."

The investigation which called this testimony from Jay Gould, was rigidly opposed by all the leading railroads of New York. Though the railroads could not entirely suppress the investigations, they could and did prevent any legislation in behalf of the people as against the railroad corporations.

The late United States Senator, David Davis, a man who always spoke, voted and acted on his principles, said:

"The rapid growth of corporation power, and the malign influence which it exerts, by combination on the National and State Legislatures, is a well-grounded cause of alarm. A struggle is pending, in the near future, between this over-grown power, with its vast ramifications all over the Union, and a hard grip on much of the political machinery, on the one hand, and the people in an unorganized condition, on the other, for control of the government."

Mr. Davis was right; a struggle is pending. If the people knew it; if the people could see the design of these men, there would be no need of fear, but alas! many of the people have little time or disposition to think.

Mr. Thurber, at one time the efficient president of the Anti-Monopoly League, sums up an immense amount of history in the following:

"In 1877 the great railroad riots took place, and, at Pittsburg a large quantity of railroad and other property was destroyed. The railroad company refused to indemnify shippers, but at the same time had bills introduced in the Pennsylvania Legislature to make the State responsible to them. They employed lobbyists to buy these bills through the legislature, but their operations were exposed and William H. Kemble, E. Petroff and others, were arrested, tried, and notwithstanding extraordinary efforts were made to secure their acquittal, were convicted. They immediately applied for pardon and were pardoned."

If I remember correctly, some of them never went to prison at all, others were in prison only four days. Hon. Freeman O. Willey concludes his admirable argument on this subject as follows:

"The next blood-curdling thought which I would have linger in the mind of the reader is, that so far-reaching and potent is the political influence of the railroads in this government, that if, perchance, any of their agents are found guilty of crime, as in the case of Kemble and Petroff, United States Senators can leave their places in the Senate, and while drawing pay from the people, for their services, can use their time and influence to secure the pardon of criminals who have bribed the people's representatives, and still retain their positions as leaders of a great political organization, that boasts of its morality, patriotism and intelligence. I would have you remember, also, that the Associated Press did not condemn those senators, and made no attempt to strengthen the arm of Palmer and Stone, who were standing by the people in refusing to pardon the villians who had been poisoning the very life-blood of the Republic."

I could give pages of testimony on this case, but this is enough. The statements above made show that we, as a nation, are sinking down in the depths of sin so deep that the query forces itself upon those who read "the signs of the times:" Can we save ourselves from ourselves? Heaven help us to open our eyes!

CHAPTER VII.

HAVE WE A REPUBLIC?

The text for this department of my sermon,
comes from Henry George.

"The true Republic is not yet here; but her birth-
struggles must soon begin. Already with the hope of
her, mens' thoughts are stirring. Not a Republic of
landlords, and peasants, nor a Republic of millionaires
and tramps; not a Republic in which some are masters
and some serve; but a Republic of equal citizens, where
competition becomes co-operation, and the inter-dependence of all, gives true independence to each.
Where moral progress goes hand in hand with intellectual progress, and material progress elevates and
enfranchises even the poorest and weakest and lowliest."

My first duty is to analyze my text.

64

1. "The true Republic is not here." How could it be here? Our government was merely an experiment—an experiment entered into by those who had had no experience whatever in conducting governments. Up to this time their whole duty had been to obey laws, not to formulate governments. It was much the same as it would be for landsmen who never saw the ocean, to undertake to run one of the Cunard steamers from New York to Liverpool; they possibly might get there, but they surely could not be considered scientific navigators of the sea.

Our fathers, with no experience, and with no model before them, undertook to formulate a government. To me the wonder is that they could do as well as they did. They made a good start; had we, their sons, improved on the model they left us, we might to-day live in the enjoyment of a genuine Republic.

In a true republican form of government, every man, and for that matter every woman, on exactly the same conditions, can walk up to the polls and vote for the men and women of their choice for all the offices in the gift of the people, and there will be no other offices, and while minorities would seldom if ever fail of being represented, majorities would rule.

Such is not the case in this country. We are soon to enter upon a political campaign. Who cares

5

for the vote of the State of Iowa, Nebraska or Kansas on that occasion? No one. Why? Because all these States are safe for one party, and whether that party gets the votes of these States by two hundred votes or two hundred thousand, makes no practical difference. The vote, not of the people, but of the electoral college is what parties are after. Ten times as much will be spent to gain the *fifty-six* electoral votes of New York as will be spent in any other five States of the Union. Why? Because the one who gets these *fifty-six* votes will be the president whether the people of these *forty* great States say so or not. That is not republicanism.

Even if the people could vote directly for the ones they want to fill the offices of president and vice president during the next four years, we have not even then a republican form of government. The majority do not vote for the candidates of their choice as they would in a genuine Republic. A very small minority shapes the policy of parties, brings out their candidates and delivers the voters over to the party and to the candidate nominated.

The history of almost any political convention tells the story. Each delegation from each district of each State, goes "instructed." A hundred candidates may be before a convention, the parties of each swearing that they never will allow any body else except their candidate to be nominated,

then all kinds of wire-pulling and intrigues are in-
augurated and the fight goes on in earnest, until
one, and sometimes all the candidates are whipped
out of the field. A new one, unthought of before,
is brought out and as the bitter partizans cannot
agree on any of the others, the "dark horse" is nominated as a spite to all other candidates except ours.
Thus Hayes and Garfield were both nominated because nobody wanted them, and elected because
people were "whipped in," to vote for candidates
they did not want.

When a candidate is once before the people he
becomes the candidate of a party, and, good or
bad he must be lauded by his party, and, good or
bad, he must be denounced as the worst man on
earth by those not of his party.

Again, in this country, majorities seldom elect.
I remember an election in Massachusetts, in 1876,
I believe. I was a citizen of that State at that time
and commented, in my paper, on the circumstance.
There were eleven men to elect to Congress and there
were five political parties in the field, each of which
nominated eleven men. The Republicans nominated and elected *eleven* men, casting less than three-
sevenths of the entire vote of the State. The Dem-
ocrats cast two-sevenths of the votes and elected nobody; the remaining two-sevenths of the votes were
divided among Greenbackers, Prohibitionists and

Woman Suffragists. As far as effecting anything was concerned over *four-sevenths* of the votes were thrown away. In a republican form of government, if a certain party casts *three-sevenths* of the votes they would have *three-sevenths* of the offices; the others would have their *pro rata* of offices. If such were the case, Congress could never divide up into two great parties and every man feel compelled to go with his party, right or wrong. Every man would be his own party, and we would, as a result, have wise legislation. As it is, votes to-day are merchantable commodities, both in and out of legislative bodies.

2. Mr. George continues: "Her birth-struggles must soon begin." So they must, or we are to lose the little semblance of republicanism we still claim. Men are to-day thoroughly dissatisfied with the way things are going. There is a greater inquiry into the cause of the evils under which we suffer, and this inquiry is educating the masses as never before. To-day many common laborers are investigating questions of political economy; and some of them are asking questions their members of Congress cannot answer.

Politicians are fearing the people as they never did before. The people have a taste of independence; they are reading the daily and weekly papers and are more inclined to vote independently, and to watch their public servants than they ever were in the past. The politician feels that he is being watched and is making more of an effort to cover his tracks than he ever did in the past.

3. "A Republic of equal citizens"—"not of millionaires and tramps."

With corporations endowed with almost infinite power and their lives lasting centuries, it will be impossible to maintain a Republic. Under such circumstances we are not born equal—one is born "with a silver spoon in his mouth," and another is born his slave. Under such conditions, the right to sin, suffer and starve, are the only rights really guaranteed to the masses. Nothing short of a Republic of equal citizens can ever be called a Republic; a government which fosters and fattens corporations at the expense of its men brings upon itself its own doom. A Republic of equal citizens cannot be a *man's* government; it must recognize woman's citizenship and her rights as a citizen. Until I and my wife can walk to the polls, side by side, and each deposit our ballot for the men and women of our choice, to fill the offices, we have no Republic of equal citizens.

4. Competition must give place to co-operation. Every man must consider every other man his brother, and must treat him as such; that will end the capital and labor struggle; it will end our tedi-

ous and expensive court wars, and every able-bod-
ied person will earn, and thus insure their own living. Every person will feel his dependence on
every other, and this grand inter-dependence will,
indeed, make one family of us.

5. One thing more will be required to make us
all we should be; that, Mr. George expresses thus:

"Where moral progress joins hand in hand with intellectual progress, and material progress elevates and
enfranchises even the poorest, and the weakest and the
lowliest."

Capital to-day has subsidized the best intellect
and talent in every department of life. When intellect becomes thoroughly moral, then it will address itself to the elevation of the weakest and the
lowliest. Henry George is seconded in his statement that "the true Republic is not yet born," by
Col. B. S. Heath, who said:

"The revolution of '76 is not yet completed, the Republic is not yet born. The efforts of our fathers, like
those of too many of the present day, were for reform,
simply. They appealed for redress of grievances.
The blood that flowed at Concord and Bunkerhill was
not for liberty and independence, but for temporary relief. The war of the Revolution was not, at first, waged
against the system of monarchy, but against the sever-
ity of the monarch."

These men are both right; we have, as yet, no
Republic, our lack in that direction is partly de-
picted by Dr. Shellhouse, as follows:

"This government is not a Republic; it is a government of landlords and tenants, of millionaires and paupers, of masters and slaves. It is a government of golden splendor, of pomp and display, and of miserable obscurity; of purple and fine linen, and debasing rags; of crime and misery in high places, and of misery and crime in low places; with prisons filled and lunatic asylums overflowing; crime, insanity and suicide increasing, drunkenness and debauchery sapping the foundation of moral purity, and threatening the overthrow of society and domestic institutions;—these are the results of inordinate wealth in the hands of a few.'

This is enough, at present, on this subject. The evils spoken of in the above quotations must be remedied or the American eagle must fold her wings and die. The question now presents itself: How will these evils be remedied? I answer, the first element of this remedy must be in a proper education of the people. Without education—particularly in certain directions—the people never can sustain a democratic Republic. Every child born in the country should be educated as to the meaning of our institutions; they should be so educated that they would be qualified to fill any position they may be called to act in, from constable up to president.

For this, a thorough business education, and a political education is necessary, but a religious education is unnecessary. An individual could be a member of any church, or of no church, and perform all his duties toward his fellow citizens, as a citizen, or as an officer in this government. The children are born for the State, to fill any position in the State to which they may be called. It is, therefore, plainly the State's duty to qualify them for what may be expected of them. If parents wish their children educated in any particular department of religion, they have a right, at their own private expense, to give them that education. No one has a right, however, to compel another to send his children to a sectarian school, or even to listen to prayers or the reading of Bibles or Korans in our common public schools. The State and the Church must, for the good of both, be kept entirely separated.

Our government is a compact for self-protection —a necessary evil. It is in no sense an association for the promulgation or the furtherance of any religious sentiment.

I would, therefore, urge that every citizen of this government must have a plain common school business education, and then that they must have an opportunity to be educated on every act of our National and State Legislatures, and every political movement in this country. I, therefore, repeat the plea which I have been making for almost a generation, that, by some means a record of all that is done by States or by the federal government should be put into the hands of every voter in the land.

This could be done by no other means so well as

by compelling every post-office in the United States, to keep on file, and for examination, a complete record of every word that is said and of every vote that is taken in Congress.

As matters are to-day, the common people know very little of what their representatives are doing. Newspapers cannot always get the truth, if they would, and many of them would not, if they could. Postmasters have often suppressed the very news which should have been carried to every voter in America. I am old enough to remember when postmasters in the South suppressed the New York *Tribune.* Those suppressed papers probably contained the very things the people of the South most needed to know—the things which might have prevented them from rushing hot-headedly into a mad rebellion, the effects of which placed the hand of progress for the South nearly a century back on the dial plate of time.

As matters have been, government has assisted both the North and the South to a misunderstanding of each other. When Col. Hayne, of South Carolina, and Daniel Webster, of Massachusetts, had their famous debate, each man's speeches, under his frank, went to his constituency. The speeches of neither man reached the other senator's constituents; thus, the South Carolina senator could misrepresent New England and the entire North

in his speech; the Southerners got their lessons of
the North from their honorable senator. On the
other hand, the North which did not get Hayne's
speech, got representations of it through Webster's
reply; thus, the North did not get its lessons either direct or correct. The result was, the differ-
ences went on, each party knowing really only one
side of the matter until it culminated in the war
which cost both the North and the South so much
blood and treasure.

Now, had Col. Hayne known that his speech
would be forced into every post-office in the North,
for the inspection of every citizen, would he have
made it? Probably he would, but its tone would
have been vastly different from what it was. Webster, also, would have known his reply was to be
read by every man and woman in the South who
cared to read, and thus he would have said some-
things he did not say, and have left out many things
he did say.

This is true of every debate that comes up in
Congress. Every congressman would know that
people could not be deceived about his speeches,
votes and drunks. The result would be that many
of them would conduct themselves differently from
what they now do. Thus, at a very small cost, the
nation would be educated to know its wants and
what it is getting. Every time a congressman of-

fered them stones for bread, they would know it; the result would be, instead of our public servants deceiving us, and riding booted and spurred over the people to wealth and power, the people would elect all such men to stay at home.

I would urge as the next consideration to bring about a genuine Republic, the abolition of the appointing power. I urge that first, because that is Republicanism. Why should I, a Republican, be compelled to send to Washington and ask a stranger there if he will permit my neighbor, Brown, Jones or Smith to handle my mail? Why have I not as good a right to help elect my postmaster as to assist in electing the village constable? If it is Republicanism for our president or our member of Congress to appoint our postmaster, why is it not Republicanism for him to appoint our school-board, the mayor of our village or our road supervisor? Where is the necessity of going through the farces of elections if we must submit to have some political tool put in over us to handle our mail? If it is not republican to allow a potentate or autocrat in Washington to appoint all of our officers, why is it republican for him to appoint any of them?

The evils of the appointing power are too numerous to be even hinted at here. The eloquent Freeman O. Willey, in his "Whither are we Drifting?" has the following language:

"Is more argument needed to prove the great wrong-fulness, danger and despotism of the appointing system? It gives the partizan and politician power to reward his friends for dirty work, in political campaigns, from the public treasury. It gave General Grant an opportunity to appoint partizan friends and relatives to office, even down to the remotest cousin, and induced him to make a desperate attempt to violate a time-honored custom, that he might make A. T. Stewart (who had given him a house at Long Branch,) Secretary of the American Treasury. It gave Rutherford B. Hayes, an opportunity to bribe men to count him into the presidential chair, with a promise of an office, as a reward for the dastardly deed. If it be urged that Grant and Hayes did not appoint men to office from unworthy motives, it is enough to say that *the appointing system gave them the opportunity to do so.* It is charged against them, and truth compells me to add, that many a man has been hung on testimony less positive than that which their accusers have produced, to sustain the charge. The fact that the appointing system gives the president the power to appoint unworthy partizans to office, and to set bad men to rule over the people without their consent, is enough to condemn it in a free government. Indeed the government is not free where such a system exists."

Next, I insist that before the genuine Republic can come, the veto power must be taken from the president. To the people, in Republics, should be the final appeal. Before our government was formulated a great writer said:

"Congress must not be permitted to make laws; only to propose, and the people to ratify them."

In the next chapter the remedy for some of the evils spoken of in this chapter will be proposed.

CHAPTER VIII.

WHERE IS THE REMEDY?

The remedies for the evils spoken of in our so-called Republic may not all be stated in this book, but as I have already hinted at some of them I will mention a few more of the remedies here.

I said, "the veto power must be taken from the president of the United States," I now say we have no use for such a superfluity as a president.

It is said the time was when the Russian government kept a live bear, at the government's expense, and many thought the government could not exist without a bear; it always had a young bear in training so that if anything should happen to the government bear his place could be supplied immediately. Once upon a time the old government bear froze to death; the weather was such that it was several days before his place could be supplied; it was noticed that the wheels of government moved on just the same, the bear had been an expense but of no actual service to the government; the government bear was abolished, since which time the government has got along better than ever before. If some of the other useless government clogs, called officers, could be frozen out the government would be the gainer in the operation.

Now it costs more to make a president every four years, and to keep him than it would cost to keep ten thousand bears and he is of no more use to the government than a bear would be in his place.

We have argued that the appointing power should be taken from the president—that every officer should be elected by the people; now, if Thomas Paine was right when he said: "Congress must not be permitted to make laws; only to propose them, and *the people* [not the president,] *to ratify them*," then there will be little left for the president to do—in fact, nothing that cannot as well be done by a congressional committee.

Our president is an expensive bear. His salary of *fifty thousand* dollars a year and mansion and furniture found him, enough to pay the wages of a hundred honest, intelligent and hard working

laborers, is the smallest part of the cost to the people of a president. A million of dollars in money
and two more millions in time spent will not cover
the expense of saying who shall be our president
the next four years. This useless expenditure of
money would go a great way toward relieving the
distress in this country.

When the office of president is gone there will
be little room for the third house of Congress,
known as the lobby, to get in its mischief. The
lobbiest had always much rather bulldoze one
man than a whole Congress. To illustrate, see
how the lobby of bankers, killed the "Legal Tender
Act," so as to make a law intended for the benefit
of the people in the time of the war, the most oppressive measure ever enacted in this country. See
how another lobby of bankers convened in Philadelphia, and got General Grant there, once upon a
time and made him veto a law which he himself
had asked Congress to pass—a law restoring to the
people the money illegally taken from them, thus
bringing bankruptcy to nearly a whole nation.
The influence of the lobby owned the president in
that one case, and the influence of the bankers over
Rutherford B. Hayes during his assumption of an
office to which he was not elected, has cost the
people of this country more than the war.

I submit that the office of president costs the

country entirely too much; it is too great a lever
for evil, to be put into any one man's hands and
there is too little good to be derived from it; let us
cut it down as a cumberer of the ground.

When the office of the president is abolished and
the veto power is put into the hands of the people,
where it belongs, our congressmen, being responsible to the people and having to answer directly to
them will be put in a wholesome fear of the people, which will cause them to consult the wants of
the people as they never have before.

Not only this, but the effect can but be good
for the people. They will feel, and act upon their
responsibility. The study of political economy will
be a necessity. People will be compelled to take
an interest in political matters in order to know
how to act intelligently on every recommendation
of Congress which will be handed back to them
for the final passage. The Congressional Record being kept in every post-office, people will go there
and post themselves on every movement in which
they are interested. People will feel they have
more interest in the government and will become
more active in republicanism than ever before.

Many of the bad laws passed by Congress and
signed by the president would never, under such
circumstances, have become laws.

Let me give a sample case. It is very small, I

acknowledge, but it serves to illustrate hundreds of similar cases. After President Garfield died Congress passed a bill pensioning his widow *five thousand dollars* per annum, during her life. That is a very small affair I know; it does not cost the reader or writer of this probably more than one cent per annum, but as small as it is there is a principle involved which a soldier brings out as follows:

"I am following the cultivator in small corn, and no very flattering prospects of a crop; I get, very naturally, to contrasting my condition with that of some other people, and wonder how my wife would f.el if I should be taken away—then I could not but think of Mrs. Garfield. A New York paper, speaking of Mrs. Garfield, says:

"She has $300,000 in government bonds, the result of a subscription; her husband's life was insured for $50.000, which she promptly received. She also received the president's salary for the unoccupied first year; amounting to about $20,000; then add to that $30,000, the value of Garfield's estate; that makes $400,000. Now the income from this sum will not be far from $16,000 a year. Most people would think that a comfortable income."

Now, you men that labor, take heed. After having all the doctor's bills paid, this woman is given a pension of $5,000 a year which is $13.79 every day in the year. Now, you men that plow and grub for 75 cents to $1.00 per day, study over this matter."

Many other instances as impressive as the above could be given. The bill to fasten the National Banks on us for twenty years more, signed by Mr. Hayes, never could have become a law, had it been submitted to a properly enlightened public. The re-chartering the National Banks will, during the

6

twenty years that their charters run, cost the nation
more than did the four years' war.

The argument on the expensive and useless lux-
ury of a president is summed up by Mr. Shellhouse
as follows:

"The vast powers conferred by the Constitution upon
the president has made that office the object of the most
zealous and determined pursuit, and the great parties
have become mere factions, organized for the sole purpose of profit, power and prestige; and have lost sight
of the people's interest altogether. In view of these
facts, how foolish and short-sighted it is to be carried
away by party spirit, to train under the whip of some
leader, for the sole purpose of elevating him to power."

When the office of president is abolished and the
people take into their hands the power now delegated to a president, they would soon see many of
the monopolies, now the pet of the government,
hurled from their throne. Instead of re-chartering
National Banks, something similar to the *fortieth*
demand of the Knights of Labor would be framed
into law. The demand reads as follows:

"The establishment of a National Monetary System,
in which the circulating medium, in necessary quantity,
shall issue directly to the people, without the interven-
tion of the banks; that all the national issue shall be
full legal tender in the payment of all debts, public and
private, and that *the government shall not* recognize
any private banks or create any banking corporations."

With this proposition framed into law, and another one, that money shall be loaned by the government directly to the people, on ample security

at a rate of interest, not exceeding two per cent., we will be well on the road to a permanent cure of many of the evils spoken of in former chapters.

To effect this demand of the Knights of Labor, nothing is needed but to carry out an article in our Constitution as it is:

"Congress shall have power to coin money and regulate the value thereof."

Why should Congress and the president have united to delegate that power to a corporation; and if Congress passes a law and the president signs it, delegating one of its prerogatives away, why not delegate all its other powers away, and quit business?

Among the other powers of Congress, is that of establishing post-offices and post-roads; why not give that power to another body of equally as honorable gentlemen, known as star route thieves? Its power to "declare war," could be delegated to the gunsmiths and powder makers; they know as much more about war and when we are ready for it, than the average congressman, as the banker knows about money more than he does.

Let Congress do its duty, and let the demand of the Knights of Labor be carried out; let another law be passed loaning the people money as cheaply as it is now furnished to rich banking corporations and the millennium will be here.

Capitalists will not compete with the government in loaning money at a low rate of interest, the result will be their money will be invested in productive enterprises; labor will be employed, we will no longer with our hills and valleys full of timber and our country full of idle workingmen, import our clothes-pins from China.   Our silks will no longer come from France, our knives from Sheffield, or our shawls from India.   Under these conditions our roads can all be macadamized, our wharfs built as they should be, and fine public buildings could adorn every city in the land.   We have labor enough to do this, and much more, and were we not giving the wealth of the country to corporations, would have enough, and to spare.   A wise man said:

"He that giveth to the rich shall surely come to want." —Prov. xxii:16.

"Shall the demon reign eternal
O'er this blessed land fraternal?
Shall enchantment so infernal hold us ever 'neath its spell?
No! by all the powers of heaven,
From this land he shall be driven.

Usury be hurled unshriven,
To the lowest depths of hell!
Then a mighty shout be given,
Hear the hosts their voices swell,
Labor conquers!—all is well!"

CHAPTER IX.

WHAT SHALL BE DONE WITH THE SENATE?

OUR SENATE NOT A REPUBLICAN INSTITUTION.—THE "CHECK" ARGUMENT ANSWERED.—"RIGHTS OF MAN," OBJECTIONS. —THE LEGAL TENDER ACT.—OF WHOM IS THE SENATE COMPOSED?—THE CALIFORNIA SENATE.—GOOD BILLS PIGEON-HOLED IN THE SENATE.—TENANT FARMERS THE RESULT.—OUR SPHINX QUESTION.

The United States Senate is not a Republican institution and does not belong to a Republican form of government. It is not elected by the people—is not of the people or for the people. It is simply an American House of Lords foisted on the government at an immense expense, for the benefit of monopolies. The people have no use for any law-making power they did not themselves create. Thus far our Senate has existed only to put the brakes on what would have been wise legislation. I know the argument is made that two Houses are more apt to legislate wisely than one; that the Senate can put a check on bad legislation. The difficulty is, the check is liable to be thrown in at the wrong place.

Thomas Paine said, in his "Rights of Man:"

"The objection against two Houses are, first, that there is an inconsistency in any part of a whole Legislature coming to a final determination by a vote on any matter, whilst that matter with respect to the whole, is only in train of deliberation, and consequently open to new illustrations. Second, that, by taking the vote of each as a seperate body, it always admits of the possibility, and is often the case, in practice, that the minority governs the majority, and that, in some instances, to a great degree of inconsistency. Third, two Houses arbitrarily checking each other is inconsistent, because it cannot be proved, on the principles of just representation that either should be wiser or better than the other. They may check in the wrong, as well as in the right, and, therefore, to give them the power where we cannot give the wisdom to use it, nor be assured of its being rightly used, renders the hazzard, at least equal to the protection."

I could refer to probably a hundred cases to prove that Mr. Paine was right. Take, for example, the Legal Tender Act, one of the best bills that ever passed the Lower House of Congress. When it went to the Senate, Thaddeus Stevens, said "it was loaded down with so many amendments its father could not recognize it." The original design of the whole bill was changed, and what was intended as a relief to the people, became one of the most oppressive laws ever passed.

It is well known to-day, that the Senate is a body of monopolistic tools, most of whom have purchased their seat in the American House of Lords. Any mean move that monopolists wish to have sanctioned by law can get the aid of a majority of our United States Senators at any time. The following extract from a California paper giving the status of its State Senate will apply to the House of Lords, holding its annual carousal in Washington.

"Speaking generally, the Assembly did much better than the Senate. Its record on vital issues is good. Had all the bills passed by it become laws, the rights of the people would have been better protected. The Senate has been the theatre of manipulation and of evil practices. Useful and essential legislation has in several instances been stifled."

That is the object of Senates everywhere. When the people's representatives pass good and wholesome laws the Senate generally makes it its business to "stifle" them. On this point, we could refer to a hundred instances in the United States Senate. Congress once passed a law that the lands given to railroads and forfeited by the companies by their non-compliance with the conditions on which it was given, should be restored and opened for settlement, but the Senate "stifled" the bill by pigeon-holeing it.

Had the people been the *referendum* in this instance there would not now be, as there are in America, out of *eight million* farmers, *one million one hundred and sixty-two thousand three hundred and seventy-three* of them working on tenant farms —paying fines to rich landlords for the privilege of producing the necessaries of life.

While this country is loaded with that anti-republican, and mischief-working institution, known as the United States Senate, we never can be a Republic. Instead, we must be a government, in which landlords and the landless, millionaires and misery, palaces and paupers, extortioners and extreme degradation will rapidly and inevitably increase. Rascality in the name of law will sway its iron scepter over a plundered people.

Our Sphinx is repeating the question: How can we redeem this country from rich robbers and deliver it into the hands of the honest, toiling masses? Upon our answer depends our life.

CHAPTER X.

OUR JUDICIARY SYSTEM.

NO JUSTICE FOR THE POOR IN COURTS.—HENRY WARD BEECH-
ER'S TESTIMONY.—JUSTICE HIDDEN BEHIND TECHNICALI-
TIES.—EFFORTS TO KEEP TRUTH OUT OF COURTS.—"SWEAR
AS I TELL YOU."—DISTRICT ATTORNEY CORKHILL ON THE
SITUATION.—WHERE ARE THE MISSIONARIES?—OUR JURY
SYSTEM.—AN OLD LAWYER ON THE SITUATION.—DEMOR-
ALIZING INFLUENCE OF LAWYERS AND COURTS.—COURTS
ANTI-REPUBLICAN.—JOHN SWINTON ON THE LAWYER.—
ARBITRATION.

"Go look to yon judge in his dark flowing gown,
With the scales wherein law weigheth quietly down,
Where he frowns on the weak and smiles on the strong
And punishes right, while he justifies wrong;
Where jurors their lips on the Bible have laid;
To render a verdict they've already made;
Go there in the court-room and find, if you can,
Any law for the cause of a moneyless man."

No department of our so-called republican form
of government needs making over more than our
judiciary system. It is now absolutely out of the
question for a poor man to get anything bordering
on justice in any of our courts. In courts money
moves everything as it does everywhere else. Henry
Ward Beecher never preached a more truthful sermon than when he said:

"All the frame-work of society seems to be dissolving.

On every side we find men false to the most important trusts. *Even judges on the bench are bought and sold like meat in the shambles.* One must go into court with a long purse to obtain justice. The judiciary of New York stinks like Sodom and Gomorrah. * * *' It is no longer an honor to sit on the bench, for, if the judge be an upright man his character will be contaminated by the great majority of his associates."

Think of a poor man obtaining justice in lawing with rich corporations; the idea is preposterous! Courts are ordained to hide justice behind what is called technicalities. Anybody can understand justice but nobody can understand law as it is; and, when an attorney is employed, his business is to cover up, to meet technicality with technicality, to obscure and not to bring out facts individually. I have kept away from courts as much as possible; but on a few occasions I have been summoned as a witness; I never went that I did not feel that I wanted to tell the whole truth about the matter; I wanted to see difficulties between neighbors adjusted with as little friction as possible; yet, if I ever succeeded in getting the truth before a court it was in spite of two paid sharpers who were there to prevent witnesses telling the truth. The first thing on the program is to swear a witness to tell the truth, the whole truth, and nothing but the truth. Then when he begins, one side or the other forbids his telling that, and lawyers and judges banter and quarrel until a modest witness is usually so confounded that he hardly knows what he is saying.

We once heard a lawyer privately telling a witness what she must and what she must not swear. The witness said: "But the thing you wish me to swear is false." "That is no difference," said the attorney, "The gaining of our case depends upon your swearing as I tell you." She swore as she was instructed and the "scales of justice," were turned by her false oath.

At the trial of the Creek murder case, in the city of Washington, District Attorney Corkhill said:

"I cannot allow this case to pass without calling attention to the remarkable exhibition of want of character of the witnesses, both for the government and the defense. In this case, and in the one tried a few weeks ago of a similar character, almost one hundred witnesses had been examined; *and so much perjury and utter disregard of the obligations of an oath* I never saw in a court of justice. It suggested to me that those worthy and benevolent gentlemen and ladies who are soliciting money and devoting their time to reforming the heathen. from Greenland to Africa, can find work closer home, here at their own Capital. If these one hundred people represent the neighborhoods in which they live, under the very dome of this temple of justice, and within the sound of the church bells, there is a field ripe for harvest, as worthy the laborer; and as fully demanding his attention, as any to be found in the sands of Africa or on the shores of Abyssinia."

These liars may not have been made to lie by the attorneys, yet, with attorneys and judges opposed, it is hard to tell the truth.

Our jury system is in one sense of the word as bad and anti-republican as it can be. Jurymen must either be knaves enough to swear themselves on the jury by swearing their incompetency for such a place, or they must swear themselves ninnies taking no interest in matters of daily occurrence.

Samuel Sinnett, an old and able lawyer of this State, exposes our judiciary system as follows:

"There is no place where reform is more loudly called for than in our courts of law. It is strange that in the latter part of the nineteenth century the demand for reform in courts has not been treated with that respect to which such a subject is entitled. But, instead of keeping up with the spirit of the age, and repealing old obsolete laws and rulings in our courts, we are piling up a pyramid of absurd and complicated, contradictory statutes, that are victimizing all those who seek justice in our courts. Fully four-fifths of the people are in favor of courts of arbitration (where no lawyers should be allowed to plead), where cases might be tried on their merits, and justice rendered without such fearful costs and the torture of prolonged delay, and the rude and often insulting remarks of the cross-questioning of the counsel, who often treat witnesses as if they were in the habit of perjury.

Then our whole system is wrong. The idea of one man deciding a case where eleven are in favor of conviction might have done very well in the days of John Calvin, but it is altogether out of place in the present age. Why not have a two-thirds majority render a verdict."

"The Grand Jury is a relic of a past age, which, like the Electoral College and the Senate ought to be sent up to the garret with the rest of the lumber. But some will ask, "what should become of our lawyers?" They could not all be sent to Congress and the Legislature; your system would simplify justice; and there would be but little chance for prolonged litigation! When were our laws honestly executed (bad as some of them are)? There would not be such cause for complaint; but we find our courts have become mere skinning establishments, where the flaying is continued as long as there is hide enough left to pay for the operation.

You can't give a simple note-of-hand any more without there is an iron-clad provision to pay a reasonable attorney's fee, (generally from $50 to $100, when $5.00 would be ample pay for the service,) and then costs are all secured by provisions of the note. But worst of all is the iron-clad mortgage, with its coupons each and all claiming like fees and costs! I know of one firm that has loaned out five millions of *Scotch Capital* on mortgages on farms (these money-lenders always prefer that class of property), the principal and interest coupons all to be repaid in gold at a certain Banking House in New York. What a fat thing this will be for the lawyers that collect them! Now, this is always loaned on a valuation of one-third, so that there is a rich margin to fatten on. And yet those very farmers will vote for lawyers to represent them, expecting those men to make laws to protect the people from such a system of things. What fools the lawyers are to neglect their own interests! Now, the worst class of men to send to Congress and the Legislature to make laws, are, without exception, lawyers, because they have no interest in common with their constituents, and will make the laws as mysterious and contradictory as possible.

It is generally believed, that judges are seated on the bench to administer justice agreeable to law, and in harmony with the Constitution. as it is generally conceded that no statute can be of force when it conflicts with the Constitution. I will here relate a little of my own experience in that respect.

We had one of these legalized robbery schemes enforced here, termed a five-per-cent. tax, to aid in building a railroad. A number of the tax-payers refused to pay the tax, and sued out an injunction against the collector forbidding him selling our property. (Just imagine: selling our homes out, to build a railroad to rob us!) Well, they sent for a certain judge from a neighboring county to come and try the injunction suit. In rendering his decision, he made use of the following singular statement: That there was little doubt but that *the law was unconstitutional.* Private property shall not be taken for public purposes without just compensation (U. S. Court); but there was a *decision* by which he would have to be governed, and he dissolved the injunction and ordered our property to be sold. The judge that had so just a respect for the decision of a court, and so little for the Constitution, has since been advanced to the Supreme Bench, where his decisions will become law for future aspiring pettifoggers.

I will here state another case to show how justice is carried on in our courts. A certain young man committed forgery for some trifling amount. The penalty was only three months in the penitentiary. He wanted to plead guilty, but certain limbs of the law saw a good chance for a hand, and persuaded him to stand a trial. Well, he was indicted for the offense, and the State Attorney drew up sixteen different charges or counts in the indictment, for which he charged sixteen different fees against the county: and as the prisoner had no money to hire counsel, the judge appointed one of the bar to defend him, for which he was entitled to a $10.00 fee, but he brought in a bill of $160.00, being $10.00 for each count in the indictment. That man is one of the law-makers of Iowa, and the prosecuting attorney is before the people for election again, with a good prospect of success."

It would seem that the above leaves little to be said, except to ask why this monster of iniquity is allowed to continue? As a means of justice it is universally pronounced a failure. The moral influence of the courts of law is degrading. The ability of the legal profession is not doubted, but the profession itself as it is conducted, is morally degrading. Misrepresentation, cunning and chicanery are their tools of trade. Falsehood—sworn falsehood is not an uncommon weapon in the hands of the attorney. This spirit of cunning passes from lawyer to client, and from the client to his honor until deception is generally the rule, not the exception. The influence of the legal profession in the affairs of State is almost omnipotent. Thus government is run, not in the interest of the "common people," but in the interest of immense corporations, who are the clients of these legal gentlemen.

Our courts through and through are anti-republican. Their dictation overrides all the rights of the people. A plain statement of truth is as apt as anyway to be "contempt" and subjects the witness to such fine as "his honor" may dictate.

As for the average lawyer no man has painted him as he is, "wrinkles and all," as has John Swinton. The quotation is lengthy, but very interesting. Here it is:

"In the business of subverting the liberties of our beloved country, I do not dread the soldier with his rifle, nor the conspirator with his mask, nor the fool, nor the fanatic, nor the demagogue, nor the king in his regalia, nor the cleric with his tongue, nor the editor with his quill, nor Satan with his horns, nor yet the millionaire with his millions, if they have but a fair field. The man to be dreaded in this Republic is the shystering lawyer; legal machination is the thing of menace and danger. It is in this country especially, that the people need to be on the alert against legal quibblers; it is here they swarm, as they do nowhere else on the globe, not only in the courts, but in Legislatures and their lobbies, and every place of power and greatness.

How often, in searching amid the ruins of popular properties in other countries that once enjoyed them, do we come upon the tracks of the false lawyer! For what oppressor has he not found a legal subterfuge? For what deed of guilt has he not been ready to erect a legal bulwark? Do we not find him with a legal defense of every usurpation of every usurper; with a legal justification for any invasion of every birthright of man; with a legal quibble over every great popular franchise; with a legal glaze for every clear word of freedom; with legal pettifoggery against every establishment of right; with a legal weapon for nullifying every victory of progress; with a legal jimmy, as Major Haggerty lately said in the Assembly, to pry open every man's safe; with a legal mechanism for tearing out every stone in the fabric of justice, and for rearing every pillar in the edifice of wrong?

Not a guilty deed has ever been perpetuated by power; not a base treason has ever been hatched against the commonwealth; not a device has ever been set for the subversion of any popular right—but the false lawyer has stood ready to uphold it with the armament of false legality. He battered the Twelve Tables of Rome, he made of no effect the Ten Commandments of Moses, he stifled the genious of Magna Charta, and he is now scuttling the Constitution of the United States."

In view of the above, and a thousand other facts, we demand that the people be delivered from the power of lawyers and the courts. Arbitration can always secure justice, and generally at one-tenth of the cost of time and money expended in the courts.

CHAPTER XI.

CONCLUSION.

OBJECT OF WRITING.—HAVE WE A RIGHT TO SAVE OURSELVES?—
THE RESULTS OF ATTEMPTING TO POINT OUT A BETTER
WAY.—WHAT THE DECLARATION SAYS.—MONOPOLIES HAVE
NO RIGHTS HERE.—TYRANNY NOT EASILY CONQUERED.—
NOW IS THE TIME TO WORK.—"WHAT CONSTITUTES A
STATE?"—AN IDEAL REPUBLIC.—IT MUST COME.

In these feeble papers, written "on the fly," I have
not pointed out all the dangers which threaten our
Republic. My determination was to set the reader
to thinking, not to go into an exhaustive argument
on any point. As I look the matter over I acknowledge my heart grows sick. I ask the question again:
Can we save ourselves? or has our journey hellward
gained such momentum that it cannot be stopped?
Our Sphinx is seriously propounding the question:
How can we restore and save our civilization?

Another question is coming to the front; that
is: Have we a right to remedy the evils already
pointed out? Whoever dare attempt this, will be
pointed out and possibly hanged as an anarchist.
Capital and corporations will take every advantage
of the public prejudice. A toadying public press

will vilify and slander the one who stands up for the people's rights. The attorneys described in the last chapter will take large fees to make reform and reformers appear odious, and courts will decide against them, while they have no backing except the moral backing of being on the side of the right.

That we have a right to remedy these evils there can be no doubt, the Declaration of Independence says:

"That when any form of government becomes destructive of these ends, [the rights endowed by the Creator, of life, liberty, and the pursuit of happiness] it is the right of the people to alter or abolish it."

If that is so, we have a right to remodel this government and make it what the fathers intended it should be, a republican form of government. Every day makes monopoly stronger; every day takes from him that hath not, and gives to him that hath. Shall we arise in the strength of a virtuous manhood and prove ourselves the worthy sons of those who, at the expense of their lives wrested our institutions from King George and his banditti.

Monopolies have no more right to usurp the throne and ride rough shod over the people in this country, than King George had in 1776. The sacredness of what is called "vested rights," is no more to be regarded than was the "divine right" of kings. The "vested" king is an usurper, as much so as was George III. In the Revolution of one hundred years ago, ministers with Wesley at their head plead for the right of kings to monopolize the freedom of this country; so in the new crisis which is now upon us we will find that "tyranny, like hell, is not easily conquered," but

> "They have rights who dare maintain them,
> Time makes ancient good uncouth."

If our rights are to be secured, nay, if they are not to be taken from us, now is the time; the people should arise as one man and save the country from monopolistic sharks. Both Thomas Paine and Thomas Jefferson disputed the right of one generation to in any sense mortgage the next generation. We have a right to repudiate the bad acts of our fathers; if this were not so progress would soon come to an end.

The poet asks:

> "What constitutes a State?
>   Men, high minded men,
> With powers as far above dull brutes endowed,
>   In forest, brook or den.
> As beasts excel rocks and brambles rude;
>   Men who their duties know,
> But knowing their rights,
>   And knowing dare maintain;
> Prevent the long aimed blow,
>   And crush the tyrant,
> While they rend the chain,—
>   These constitute a State."

I see an ideal Republic—a Republic of equal citizens, where there shall be no rich, no poor, no master, no servant, but where justice shall rule and man shall be to man a brother.

"Aye, it must come! the Tyrant's throne
    Is crumbling with our hot tears rusted;
The Sword earth's mighty have leant on,
    Is cankered, with our best blood crusted.
Room! for men of Mind make way;
    Ye robber Rulers, pause no longer.
Ye cannot stay the opening day;
    The world rolls on, the light grows stronger,
        The People's Advent's coming.

www.ingramcontent.com/pod-product-compliance
Lightning Source LLC
Chambersburg PA
CBHW032200010726
47493CB00008BA/2763